# Two Suitors

# Two Suitors

by

## Younoussa Segda

# Contents

# Preface

*An old man dying is more than a library going up in flames. Among the sources of history, orality plays an important role in the knowledge of the past.*

*The tales, for their part, are an inexhaustible source of richness of the lived and the social morals of the facts of the past of those who preceded us. In a society in conquest of social value, the tales illustrate themselves as the best remedy to the agony of the moral in our societies, today dominated by corruption, treason, and so on.*

*The collection of tales is a work of updating social values which, even if upon first sight, they do not seem to provide us with the material and carnal needs of this world, how many times insatiable, leads us to the elevation of self.*

# The Two Suitors

At that time, the monkey and the chameleon decided to marry the daughter of a butcher.

Each one of them had his own position. The girl's father, who was aware of this, called the two suitors to his house.

"I will give my daughter to the first among you who catches me early in the morning," said the father.

On these words, the monkey observed the chameleon for a long time.

"What a pity!" Said the monkey, "You have no strength. Go and rest."

The chameleon was vexed and immediately started to work. He went into the bush, crying, looking for a solution. He knew that the monkey was faster than he was. The game was lost. This made him sad.

He met the doe who asked him the cause of his sorrow, and he told her his adventure. The kindly doe went to the hawk, who had long wanted to catch the monkey, then said to the chameleon.

"Dry your tears. Come with me to the village."

As soon as they arrived, they were received by the villagers. Each one explained his idea, and fortunately, with the help of their hosts, they were satisfied.

The hawk carried the chameleon on his head. The hawk and the chameleon arrived. The butcher saw the chameleon and said:

"You are a good and quick man. I will give you my daughter."

When it was already daylight, the monkey still did not decide to go to get his wife. That day, he had left his home at seven in the morning to chat with his companions.

When he arrived at "Koass-Tenga", he found the chameleon and many other chameleons gloating. All the chameleons burst out laughing and the monkey, ashamed, went home crying.

# The Cat and The Mouse

*One day, the mouse sent her little mouse to the market to buy some butter. Unfortunately, on the way, he met the cat, who asked him:*

*"My little one, where are you going?"*

*"My mother sent me to buy butter", replied the mouse.*

*"So, hurry up and get there, or you won't get the butter", said the cat.*

*With a flick of his paw, the mouse ran straight to the place. Meanwhile, the mean cat was waiting for him in the middle of the road on the way back.*

*When he arrived at the market, the mouse bought what he wanted, and at the end of the day, he carelessly took the road back to his home. On the way, he met the cat again, who blocked his way.*

*The naughty cat complained and said:*

*"Give me the butter so that I can take it to your mother. You are not fast enough, and the sun may melt it."*

*On hearing these words, the mouse wanted to run away, but the cat jumped on him and devoured him.*

*Moral:*

*Children need more protection because a failed education cannot be repeated.*

# The Dishonest Traveler

*A long time ago, a man went on a journey. His name was Nassoukou.*

*On the way, exhausted by the long journey, he decided to spend the night at a friend's house. He was going to continue his journey the next day. Fortunately for him, his friend welcomed him in to his house with his wife. That some day, a large dog was slaughtered. Nassoukou made it clear to his friend that he did not eat dog meat.*

*"It is my totem."*

*To prove his friendship, his friend lent him his donkey to make his journey pleasant. But in the middle of the night, Nassoukou got up and saw that the dog meat was fat. His mouth watered. Excited, Nassoukou took the meat and put it in his bag.*

*At the time when the roosters crow, he woke up immediately informed his friend of his departure. The latter wished him a very good trip. Nassoukou hung his bag on the donkey and disappeared into the bush.*

*On the way, unfortunately for him, frightened by two furious antelopes, the donkey knocked him down. The donkey headed back to his master's family unit carrying on its back the bag of meat that Nassoukou had stolen. Nassoukou stood up, covered in dust.*

*If you were in Nassoukou's place, would you agree to follow the donkey to its master's house, or would you continue your journey?*

# The Goat and The Hyena

In the past, animals in the bush could talk to each other. Each one had its problems. The lion was recognized as their undisputed leader. Unfortunately, one day, the lion got a serious disease called "hernia".

At that time, the goat was a salt peddler. The hyena was a cattle rustler.

One day, the hyena caught the goat in the bush with his salt. He said to him:

"Hello, friend goat. What are you selling?"

The goat answered calmly that he had become a salt trader.

On hearing this, the hyena was about to pounce on the poor animal, but the lion's roar brought him back to order.

To avoid the lion's anger, the hyena went to him.

"Majesty, I have just learned that a terrible disease has been tormenting you for some time. I have the solution to your problem: the goat."

On learning these words, the lion made the goat come. The hyena spoke up and said:

*"Friend goat, our king is currently ill, and to cure him, we need two goat ears, his testicles, all mixed with salt. This potion will relieve the pain he is suffering from."*

*Thinking he was playing a trick on the goat, the hyena started to laugh at him.*

*Suddenly, the goat stood and addressed the lion as follows:*

*"Majesty! I owe you a great deal of respect. Just know that the goat lied. We both went to see the marabout. Instead of two ears and two testicles of goat, I assure you that only the head of a hyena was recommended by the marabout."*

*The sentences of the goat made Bouki tremble. The lion stared at the hyena, who let out a loud cry. The lion jumped on him, and out off came his head. The goat mixed salt into the head.*

*When the lion ate the medicine, he was miraculously cured. This is how the goat managed to escape.*

*Moral:*

*He who is not safe should not laugh at one who is drowning.*

# The Good Man and The Girl

*In the most remote years, men in their majority were all afraid.*

*To undertake a tiny mission was difficult for them. Sadjo was a beautiful girl from a village called Fulbade. All the men were eagerly looking for this sweet creature. Everyone was looking for ways to approach her.*

*Fortunately, one morning, Sadjo's father gathered all the men of the village and said:*

*"I give my daughter to the man who will be able to bear a hundred strokes of the stick".*

*Upon hearing the news, all the men ran to their huts. The young Manéyam decided to go. His mother cried all day long, but Manéyam told her:*

*"Mother, dry your tears, I, Manéyam, killed a scorpion when I was a baby. Well, I will show the whole world that I am brave; I am not a bastard, but a man born of a know father and mother."*

*When he arrived in the king's court, Manéyam observed the whole assembly for a long time, then went to stand in the middle of the circle. An old man leered at him and spat saliva on the ground. Whether it was a curse or a blessing, only God knew.*

*A clown emerged from the crowd with a large stick and walked towards Manéyam. The former lifted the stick and beat Manéyam's back copiously. In a few minutes, the count was perfect, and Manéyam arose victoriously with a smile on his face. Sadjo's father had Sadjo's marriage celebrated, and young Manéyam became a husband.*

*It is thanks to the bravery of this man that nowadays there are brave men.*

# The King and His Three Sons

*A very rich and wise king went on a turn. Before he left, he called his children and entrusted them with his animals.*

*To the first, he gave three herds of oxen, to the second two herds, to the third one herd.*

*The first one took the three herds and went to the second one to squander his herd. The second, who took the two herds of oxen, did the same thing. But the third, who took a single herd, went away to raise it. The herd prospered and became one of the largest herds in the kingdom.*

*One day, the king returned from his turn. He asked them what they had done with his flock. The first one who took the three herds of oxen came up and said:*

*"Father, you have given me three herds of oxen. This is what I have earned - nothing."*

*And he showed his empty yard.*

*"What is this?" exclaimed his father in a thunderous voice. "Shut up, you scoundrel! You are a bad and foolish child".*

*The second man, who received the two herds of oxen, came up and said:*

*"Father, you have allotted me two herds of oxen. This is what I have earned - nothing."*

*And he pointed to an empty yard.*

*"What is that?" exclaimed his father in a thunderous voice. "Shut up, you scoundrel! You are a bad and foolish child."*

*Finally, the one who had been given a single herd of oxen came up and said:*

*"Father, you have allotted me a herd of oxen, and my yard has grown."*

*His father said to him:*

*"Ah well! You have done a good thing. What can I do to, well, thank you? I will entrust my kingdom to you."*

*The king ordered him to be taken to his palace. Then addressed the first two brothers.*

*"You will have the opportunity to reflect on your actions."*

*Moral:*

*He who sows the wind reaps the storm.*

# The Man and The Dog

*A long time ago, man and dog lived in perfect harmony. The dog could always communicate with his master. One day, the man's son became seriously ill, screaming night and day. No decoction could relieve him.*

*One morning, the man took leave of the dog and went to consult a deviner. The deviner urged him to wash the boy with the warm blood of a puppy. Our man returned to the village with tears in his eyes and told the dog the sad news.*

*"Okay, said the dog, since you are my master, I will give you one of my puppies to sacrifice, but you must be careful. I want you to bury his body after his death."*

*When he had finished his speech, he moved away behind the concessions so as not to witness the ordeal of his offspring. Taking advantage of this absence, the man performed the requested ritual, and miraculously his baby recovered his health. Instead of burying the puppy as agreed, the man quickly roasted the puppy and ate with his children. Only a few bones were put in the ground. When the dog returned home, he saw that the man's pup had recovered. He then turned to the man.*

*"Where is the grave of my pup that you killed?"*

*"I buried him here,"* the man replied.

*With a wrathful face, the dog quickly noticed the deception and began to dig in the ground, and to his surprise, he found only the bones of his pup. Completely excited, he then began to shout at the man.*

*"Master, you betrayed me. From now on, my mouth refuses to speak to you. I will bark at you to say good night, and I will greet you my tail."*

*And as you can see, the dog never talks to his master. His bark alone is enough. His tail always remains. His hand to welcome him.*

# The Old Man and His Son

*One day a boy went to his father and said:*

*"I want to ask you something."*

*"Go ahead, I am willing to listen to you, my only son."*

*"We need to buy a donkey to go around the world."*

*"Oh, no, my son! I stop you. Even with a car, we won't make it. The tour of the world is done with an iron bird. At least it is fast and comfortable."*

*"No, dad, I don't want an iron bird, what we need is a big red donkey with very strong hooves to cross the forests and mountains."*

*After some thought, the old man come to the conclusion that nothing in the world was better than a child - even less, an only son.*

*"So, my son, I support you."*

*Timbila, this is the old man we are talking about. He was a good farmer. He had several fields. He raised cattle. He also raised poultry.*

*Timbila filled up with twenty-five thousand cowries. He found the donkey.*

*Today, twenty-five thousand cowries shells represent one hundred fifty thousand cfa francs. Has anyone ever seen a donkey sold for that price? My goodness, how it weights.*

*The old man returned home with the donkey.*

*He presented it to his wife and son.*

*The child made a face:*

*"The donkey is beautiful! But let's not hang around too long. In three days, we have to go around the world."*

*It was the beginning of the dry season. The sky was blue, the wind was blowing everywhere. During the dry season, there is a festival in the kingdom. All the men and women were dancing. The griots beat their drums: it was the time of the great traditional festivals.*

*It was not yet time to leave. Soon after, the day arrived. The day of his departure, early in the morning, they left the village. The child climbed onto the animal. The old man followed the animal on foot. It was hot. They rode through the bush. The road was long. A month later, they arrived in a kingdom. But as soon as the men, women, and children of that kingdom ran up to them, they said:*

*"Look over there. He looks like a rude child! He sits down on a donkey. He lets an old man walk. See this behavior for yourself. It's true. Get down there, you rude boy."*

*Watching this scene, an old man remembered that in the past, no child could afford to do this for fear of being punished.*

*So, the child was speechless. He begged the old man to get on the beast.*

*"Here you go, father. The people of the kingdom are not happy. They say that I am a rude child."*

*But as soon as the old man got on the beast, they left the kingdom. They headed for another kingdom. They found an eager crowd near the city. Soon the men, women, and children of that kingdom were running to them, saying:*

"Look over there. He looks like a rude old man! He sits down on a donkey. He lets a child walk. See this behavior for yourself."

"It's true. Get down there, old man!"

The large crowd stopped in front of them. Watching this scene, an old man remembered that in the past, no old man could afford to do so for fear of being vilified.

The old man was deeply disappointed to be needlessly insulted.

"This is not a pleasant tour of the world from what I see, my son."

A tear rolled down the old man's cheek. They left, and as soon as they left the kingdom, the child calmed him with his childish voice:

"Father, what have you done?"

"I have done nothing."

"What have I done?"

"Nothing."

"Only you see, father, there is no remedy in staying there. Man is not only human being. He is selfish; he is dissatisfied. On with your life. I went around the world. We have been assured of a saying:

"Suffering always brings joy in the end."

"Your thought is very important, my so", said the old man.

The sun was high in the sky. The companions resumed their journey. Then a third kingdom was announced. Heavy drums sounded. All the hands beat the meeting.

Was there hope for life again? No. They were driven out of the kingdom. The inhabitants of this kingdom said:

"Look over there. It looks like an old man and his son. They have just been around the world. Get away from them! How could they do it, Those clever rascals, the liars of all kingdom? Tell us who you are? It's all wrong."

"We agree," replied the old man and his son.

*And the journey continued. When they returned, everything in the kingdom seemed to stop. The queen was stunned to death and closed her eyes forever. Embarrassed, the king moaned:*

*"Where shall I go, God? Can you wake my wife?"*

*The poor king. He continued to cry. All the inhabitants of the kingdom went out. They were not happy.*

*"Take me to the king," begged the child.*

*So, he went back to the palace. The old man was there.*

*"Let's go back with the donkey," said the child.*

*The king greeted the two strangers anxiously. They sat in the funeral parlor.*

*Suddenly, the donkey got up and brushed against the queen. Immediately, the queen sneezed. She opened her eyes and recovered.*

*The king congratulated him and sent his courtiers to announce the news. The king stood up and said:*

*"You are a good and brave child, you and your old man. I will entrust my kingdom to you after my death."*

*The king also asked to be given a hundred oxen and then a hundred horses. When he died, he replaced him on the throne as king.*

*The old man was pleased with this before he left one day.*

# The Leper and The Blind Man

*In a village lived two great friends. One was a leper, and the other was blind. One day, they got the information that a famous marabout lived not far from the village. They decided to go there to be treated. When they arrived, they were received by the marabout. Each of them explained their ailment, and fortunately, with the help of their host, they were cured. But before leaving, the marabout gave each of them a piece of advice not to be broken. He advised the leper not to clap after a loud laugh, or he would become a leper again. As for the blind man, he forbade him to see drunken milk. Otherwise, his illness would start again.*

*Back in the village, everyone told his wife the news, and together they organized a big party. The days passed peacefully, without incident.*

*Unfortunately, one day, the leper summoned his wife, who was jealous of his friend, and told her a secret.*

*"Panda," he confessed, "I'm going to play a nasty trick on my blind friend. He's been disrespecting me lately."*

*"Why is that?" Asked Panda. "I advise you not to dare because, you see, this blind man is open to all, and he respects me a lot."*

*"I don't need your advice," shouted the leper.*

*He sent his son to look for his friend. When his friend arrived, he handed him a stool.*

"Hold this," he said slyly to his friend. "I've made such good soup that we can have dinner together."

At that very moment, the leper opened the lid, and when his friend saw the milk, he became blind again.

Satisfied with his unworthy act, the leper shouted with joy and clapped without realizing he had just transgressed the ban. He became leper again.

They returned together to see the marabout. He asked each one to tell what had happened so that they would become disabled again.

Convinced of the leper's treachery, the marabout cured the blind man and told the leper:

"Since you have been unkind to your friend, know that your unkindness has condemned you for good. Go back to your home."

Morality: By wanting to harm others, you make yourself. Do not do to others what you will not want to be done to you.

# The Peasant and The Cripple

*A peasant named Tanga was traveling.*

*Along the way, he met an old man. This man was bedridden, and as he could not walk well, he begged the peasant to carry him. The latter accepted without any compensation.*

*But as soon as he reached the first village, the man started to scream, to purr, to shout:*

*"Thief, thief, thief. I want my donkey. save me, my donkey."*

*Soon, a crowd formed. Tanga couldn't believe his ears at all.*

*"No, that's not true. That animal belongs to me."*

*The impatient crowd began to glare at him threateningly.*

*"You, you are a thief, a dirty liar. You will give an account to the king".*

*So Tanga was dragged before the king.*

*"I want my donkey. That donkey belongs to me."*

*"It can't be yours," the king replied.*

*Seeing the situation getting more complicated by the hour, the prince stood up before the assembly and asked the old man:*

*"Since you say that this animal belongs to you, what sex is it?"*

*The man stood up, stumbled, and shouted:*

*"Donkey with two sexes! donkey with two sexes!"*

*The whole assembly laughed, and the son of the Chief said to the crowd:*

*"You can see that this man is a liar and a thief."*

*Confused and unmasked, the old man wanted to run away, but he was caught by some guards and then thrown into prison despite his infirmity. The donkey was immediately returned to its owner, who continued on his way.*

*Morality:*

*Truth always triumphs over falsehood.*

# The Abandoned Girl

*Coumba, a young woman, gave birth to a child named Tibo. A Victim of illness from birth, the little Tibo was wasting away day after day. This made life difficult for Coumba, who decided to get rid of him.*

*One morning, the young woman get up, put her baby on her back, and headed for the big forest. When she arrived, she untied the loincloth and laid the baby down near a bush. Back in the village, everyone was surprised to see Coumba without her baby.*

*Fortunately for Tibo, the génies of the forest came to her rescue. The disease that had been eating away at her disappeared. Now grown and full of charm, Tibo asked permission from her protectors to visit her mother. Her arrival at home was discreet. She went to her mother's hut where she left all her trousseau; then she set to work. She cleaned up the yard, fetched water, and made an excellent meal for her mother. In the end, she disappeared and returned to the forest.*

*In the evening, when she returned from the fields, Coumba was so intrigued that she did not know what to say.*

*"Maybe an angel from heaven came to visit me while I was away.", she concluded.*

*Every day, Tibo went to his mother's house and did all the work. Then one day, an old hunchback, Coumba's neighbord, discovered her but said nothing.. Back from the fields, she was informed of the news. The next days, Coumba closed her house and hid.*

*In the early morning, the young girl returned to the courtyard, her arms full of gifts. When she wanted to put the gifts in the shed, the mother hid the ustensils and threw herself at her, but the young Tibo, who was faster, "evaporated" into the air and went into the forest where she saw the djinns again and never returned.*

*Moral of the story:*

*Even when you give birth to a snake, you make a belt out of it.*

# Bassé the Hunter

*The Moagha legend tells.*

*A long time ago, a hunter called Bassé lived in a village. Descended from a caste of hunters, the man developed qualities worthy of this profession. That is why everyone in the region was afraid of him, even his fellow hunters. It was even said that before his grandfather died, he had protected him and entrusted him with all the secrets of the bush. Exceptionally, Bassé never returned from the hunt empty-handed. However, his real flaw was cruelty.*

*People criticized this behavior as too exaggerated and risky.*

*One Friday evening, around 4:00 p.m, while returning from a hunting trip, Bassé the hunter did not take any game. His face was sad, and he was sweating. But at the entrance to the village, he saw an old panther between two rocks. His hand went inexorably to the trigger, ready to shoot. Suddenly, an incredible scene occurred. The old panther raised its two front paws in the air towards the hunter and spoke a few words in a language of its own.*

*Without saying a word, our hunter pulled the trigger and bang! the bullet went off like a flash and hit the animal in the chest.*

*The panther went down twice and got up again, and the third time it did so, it addressed Bassé in these terms:*

*"Why are you so wicked to this point? Bassé, you are a ruthless man, you dared to kill me by refusing to forgive me. Well, an unfortunate event is going to happen to your family today as I speak to you."*

*After this speech, the animal fell and expired. Without a moment's hesitation, Bassé seized his game and made his entrance into the village. A few meters from the courtyard, he heard crying and screaming. It was his mother who had just given up the ghost. There was a red mark on her chest, and blood was running through her ears.*

*Bassé learned his lesson.*

# Kako the Young Shepherd

*The story really happened, according to the Moagha legend of Burkina.*

*Once upon a time, in a village, there lived a motherless young boy named Kako. His father then married a woman named Missomba.*

*The young boy became a shepherd and drove his sheep through the bush. He did not return home until the evening.*

*Kako was handsome, brave, intelligent, and hardworking despite his young age. All the young people in the village were afraid of him, even the notables of the palace. Every evening, some of the villagers went to his hut to get advice. This notoriety annoyed Missomba. She became more and more jealous and was eager to destroy the young shepherd. Evil practices had been carried out but without results.*

*Because of Missomba's increasing malice, Kako avoided her meals.*

*One day, in the middle of the bush, Kako was attacked by bandits, but thanks to his two dogs, he managed to rout them. A little injured, Kako returned home and noticed that his ugly stepmother was constantly laughing at his misfortune. With the help of his father, he was cured. This victory made him popular again throughout the region.*

*One Friday, around midnight, Missomba knocked on the door of the great sorcerer, Yeko, asking him to liquidate the young Kako immediately. After throwing his fortune-telling cowrie shells, he advised Missomba to go as quickly as possible to the most powerful dragon in the kingdom, in the Koumsaï river, near the green mountain. This dragon was very powerful because it could change itself into different forms without difficulty. It killed and devoured herds as well as men without mercy. Missomba begged the great sorcerer who accompanied him to the river, and after having sacrificed a red goat to the entities of the water, the dragon agreed to destroy Kako. The young shepherd used to lead his sheep to the river.*

*That afternoon, after having made his animals drink, Kako wanted to rest at the water's edge. A wind began to blow.*

*Suddenly, a huge red python appeared and threw him into the water. A real struggle started. The battle lasted a long time. In the face of the fierce struggle, the python transformer itself into a dragon and became crueler, with fire and arrows coming out of its mouth. Protected since his birth by his mother's fetishes, the young Kako proved to be indomptable before the monster.*

*Then, feeling at the end of his magical powers, the dragon wanted to withdraw, but the young shepherd whistled to call his two dogs. Immediately, they arrived and fought the evil dragon to the death.*

*Kako got out of the water and took a few steps. The sun had long since disappeared. Only the stars twinkled in the sky. His return to the village was triumphantly celebrated.*

*To thank him, the chief offered him three hundred sheep and one hundred oxen.*

*From that day on, Missomba became a good mother to young Kako.*

# Miranda and The Python

*Miranda was a beautiful girl from a village called Namasso. When she was eighteen years old, her father found her a husband.*

*"I don't want a husband with scars on his body", she said.*

*An evil python who heard this quickly went to the baobab and told him his problem. Friendship helps, so the baobab decided to give him his skin to allow him to marry her.*

*So, one morning, the python transformed into a handsome man and went to knock on the girl's door. At first, Miranda was dazzled by the man's immeasurable beauty.*

*"Ah, he's so cute", she said in her feminine voice.*

*Her father and mother were also overwhelmed, as were her nieces, uncles, and cousins. After that, the customery greetings took place.*

*On the other hand, Koura, Miranda's younger brother, passed by with a disfigured look due to the presence of this suitor. A lap hit him in his face.*

*"At least learn to respect grownups", his father shouted at him.*

*Koura got up and wiped his buttocks. The wedding was celebrated, and the people ate, drank, and danced to the rythm of the drums.*

*Three days after the festivities, Miranda followed her husband to another village. They walked for a big forest so wild that you couldn't even see the light of day. It was there that the handsome man turned into a real python.*

*"Come with me to this baobab tree," he ordered Miranda.*

*"No, no," replied the girl. "You're just a poor snake".*

*The angry python pounced on her and began to devour her. The girl cried out in distress. But no one could hear her in such a big forest. Just when it seemed that everything was over for her, a wild goose hunter appeared. The hunter ran over and bang!*

*With a blow from his club, he killed the famous reptile.*

*This is how Miranda was saved and brought back to the village. This time, instead of a man with no scars on his body, she married a wild goose hunter forever.*

*Moral of the story:*

*If you don't have what you are, you have to make do with what you have.*

# The Abandoned Orphan

*A king who had lost his mind ordered his guards to execute all orphaned children.*

*"This is the only way we can save money," he thought.*

*While the guards were walking around with the torch of death in their hands, slaughtering without mercy, one child managed to escape into the bush. Béloum was his name.*

*Back at the palace, the monarch rewarded his guards.*

*"From now on, you will be my all-purpose mercenaries," he concluded..*

*Fearful and afraid of being caught, Béloum hid in the high trees of the forest, crying. Suddenly, a genie appeared before him and said:*

*"Come on, little one, stop crying. Let's go into the baobab and cook."*

*Béloum obeyed and became the genie's inseparable friend. He was initiated into the djinn culture and was endowed with supernatural powers.*

*That year, not a single drop of rain fell in the village of Babouin. The villagers began to worry.*

*One day, Tanga, the hunter, who had scanned the sky, saw that rain was coming. He ran to huddle against a baobab tree. From there, he heard a voice singing. It's was Béloum's voice.*

*"Since the people of Babouin chased me away, I have never eaten their 'tô' or drunk their water; no one has come to look for me either. Let it rain everywhere, but not in Babouin."*

*After his song, the clouds that were full of water disappeared. A great fear invaded Tanga, who ran to the village to tell the news. The old men were quickly dispatched around the big baobab tree.*

*As the rain began to fall again, they heard the voice of young Béloum repeating the same song.*

*"Since the people of Babouin chased me away, I have never eaten their 'tô' or drunk their water. Let it rain everywhere, but not in Babouin.*

*The patriarch of the elders immediately threw down his cane, prostrated himself before the great baobab, and a small sacrifice of a goat was quickly offered to the spirits. Suddenly, the earth shook, and white smoke filled the forest. Béloum appeared. He was transported to the village under good escort.*

*The king beat a great turn and gave him rich gifts. That night, a great rain showered Babouin copiously.*

*Morality:*

*The orphan needs protection, support, and love.*

# The Man and The Shoe

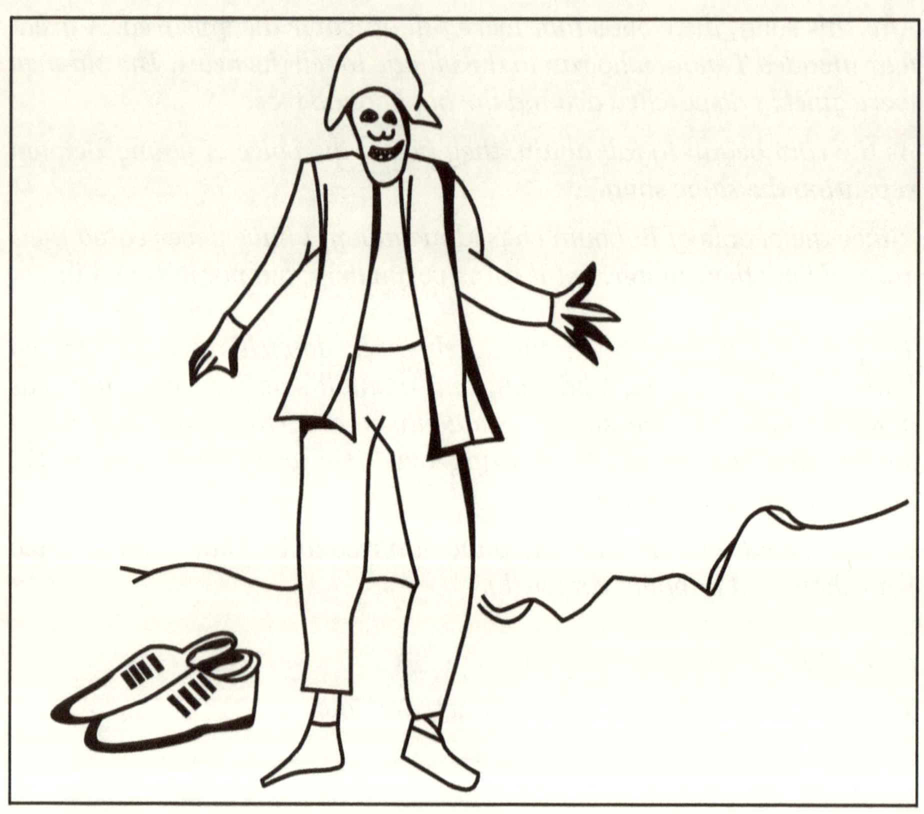

*After a long trial, a man was caught in the end.*

*In a village, a man named Napo was suspected of kidnapping a donkey. A leather shoe had been seen at the scene of the crime. The king asked a question to know more.*

*"This shoe belongs to whom?"*

*Napo laid his eyes on the king sitting in the center and said:*

*"I don't know who it belongs to."*

*Napo's father was very convincing and persuaded the king that his son was not guilty of the crime he was accused of.*

*"It is impossible, my king. You are certainly mistaken. This one is good. It is the first time that such things have happened to him. The boy hasn't taken anything for 30 years."*

*The king glanced around the room then approached Napo. He examined him carefully.*

*"It will have to be, though."*

*He was acquitted after a heated debate.*

*Then Napo turned to the king and said:*

*"Can I pick up my shoes?"*

*"This is exactly what I expected."*

*Napo was locked up under a blazing sun.*

*Moral:*

*If you're smart, you're smart; you always meet someone who's smarter than you are.*

# The Monkey and The Goat

*There was a time when the king's field was off limits. One evening, the goat and the monkey had bad luck. They were stopped by the king. The king was embraced. To refuse punishment for such serious acts was to undermine the authoritarian and legendary discipline of his kingdom. So, he decided to give everyone what they deserved.*

*"What shall I do?" he thought. "Ah, an idea! I am the king, and tomorrow, Friday, I will have the goat beaten with a rod. I will continue the second punishment. There will be a separate punishment. I will cut the tail off the monkey. You have until tomorrow to think!"*

*Scared, the goat started to cry and threw himself to the ground.*

*It was already Thursday night. When the whole palace was asleep, the goat woke up quickly. The goat cried:*

*"Ouch, ouch," he said. "I cannot move, I suffer too much. I tell you."*

*When the king and the notables rushed into the cages, the fury of the goat was at its height.*

*"Ouch, he said I cannot stay long. I suffer too much. Oh, king! Take care of my tail, I tell you."*

*The indignant king:*

*"Poor goat! what do you want?" said the king in a low voice.*

*The goat answered with a look:*

*"Ouch, ouch," he said. "Tear off the tail. Let's go quickly. I'm suffering too much."*

*"No, I don't want to," said the king.*

*"But I much," replied the goat.*

*"I'll see what I can do," said the king.*

*As soon as his tail was cut off, the goat rushed to the cage, laughed under his breath, put his head at the window, and made a gesture of contentment to the Monkey.*

*"Well, monkey, I've had a good escape! Listen, my friend, I don't mind. It's over, but you know that tomorrow you'll be beaten with a rod instead of me."*

*"My God! my God!" Cried the monkey, bursting into tears.*

*"It will be necessary," the goat replied.*

*The next day, the king received an early visit from the queen accompanied by the prince. The visit was brief. They parted cheerfully, but after the departure of the queen and the prince, the king asked urgently to release the two prisoners. The monkey greeted, smiled, and ran to tell her family, who shared her joy.*

*The goat:*

*"How is this possible? The monkey was not beaten with a rod. Never, your majesty! Never the injust punishment.*

*The king guessed the foolishness of the goat and called the hyena. But the goat ran away at full speed.*

*Which punishment is more severe? Cutting off the tail or beating the goat?*

# The Three Friends

In a village, there lived three men.

One had very thin ears, the second could see ten kilometers, and the third had a long arm.

One day, they decided to travel together to a nearby village. When they arrived, they were promptly received. Each one went his own way to get to know the world and the people better. Days passed, and one morning, they met at a ceremony in another village. The three friends took turns telling each other what they had seen and heard. But before going back to their village, they got together and bought some unhulled rice, which they put in a leather bag. They wanted to sow it as soon as they got home.

Without delay, they set off together under the hot sun. On the way, it rained, and our three friends came to a big river they had to cross. They jumped into the water, and as they crossed, a grain of rice fell. The one with sharp ears heard the noise. He called his two friends and told them. The one who could see for ten kilometers located the grain in the water. The third one plunged his hand into the river and pulled out the rice grain. All three were happy.

Which one is the greatest of the three?

# The Three Travelers

*Once, long ago, three friends from the same village decided to travel together. As they crossed the great forest, the oldest of them wanted to smoke. He took out his pipe but found that his tobacco was finished. Then he turned to his two comrades:*

*"Oh!" he exclaimed, "my tobacco box is empty. Can you help me?"*

*"With pleasure," replied the second.*

*He rummaged in his bag and gave him some tobacco leaves. The smoker retrieved them quickly but could not smoke because he had no fire. Fortunately for him, the youngest among them invented a plausible technique on the spot. With the help of two pebbles that he rubbed, he obtained a flame, and when the pipe was lit, by a miracle, a very elegant and beautiful girl came out of the smoke and fell at the feet of our three travelers. The girl radiated with all her splendor. A violent quarrel took place between the three friends. Each of them wanted to marry the girl.*

*Which of the three friends do you think should have married her?*

*For the wise man, this lady should be given to the king, morality dictates.*

# When You Love

Once upon a time, a very beautiful woman lived in a village. One day, Yébo, her husband, went to look for baobab leaves with the woman.

They travelled dozens and dozens of kilometers. They went like this through the bush. The road was long.

Finally, when they arrived, Yébo went to get the leaves. He picked as many leaves. Rabi, the woman, was there. She played with her beauty. Her hair was long and straight. She was young.

Suddenly, Rabi sang:

"Oh, I am beautiful. I am beautiful. I make men run."

Yébo was happy and said to his wife:

"Why, why do you sing?"

The woman replied:

"You didn't say you loved me."

*Yébo:*

*"So, I love you."*

*Woman:*

*"That's not enough. But it's too much to say. Come and fall into my arms."*

*Yébo opened his eyes wide and replied:*

*"You're right. I'll jump from this tree and fall into your arms."*

*"Wait until I catch you," said the woman.*

*But Yebo jumped, fell, and broke his neck. The woman was afraid. She cried and cried. She did not see her husband get up again. It was all over.*

*Love is not worth the candle. Love is not worth the effort to get it.*

# The Genius and The Poor Peasant

*In the village of Razambé lived a man called Napo. He was poor, a very poor father of two children. He lived from day to day because don't we say that every day his pain is enough? One day Napo ran out food. He then went to the forest to get some. Arriving in the forest, he saw a half-toothless old man. Napo kicked the old man.*

*"Who are you, poor old man? Clear the way, or I kill you."*

*The old man turned into a genius and said to Napo,*

*"No, my son. I am the genius of this forest. Bring me a drink rather than kill me."*

*Frightened, Napo brought him a drink. The old man cried out, "Treasure!"*

*The treasure replied, "Here I am, genius!"*

*The old man said to Napo, "Pick up the treasure. It is the gift of your ancestors."*

*Napo picked up the treasure and returned to Razambé. He became very rich the inhabitants of the village advised him to become their chief, but Napo was so nice that he preferred to remain otherwise.*

*Morality:*

*Who gives to the poor, lends to God. Whoever does charity will be rewarded late in life.*

# The Gourmand

*Salou was his name. He had made orchards where there were mango trees, banana trees, cassava, etc.*

*Salou loved to take care of the orchards. He would cut the herbs in the morning and burn them the next day. He also liked meat because it was very good. He was the biggest consumer of meat in the village. The people in the village used to reproach him.*

*"Don't talk", he said with a paunchy belly.*

*"Meat is too good. It makes me live. I know you are jealous. Come on, get out of here."*

*"Oh no. Not really", people said.*

*"The meat will kill you."*

*He said as he ate,*

*"That's what eating is all about, and why I have animals."*

*One day, Salou cut a bush. What a misfortune! A snake stung his hand. He fell and did not move. A peasant who was passing by intervened at once. The farmer killed the snake first. He took Salou to the village. The healer had a snake soup prepared and found the product. As soon as Salou ate the contents, he was cured.*

*"I want the soup", he said.*

*"The soup went well to my stomach."*

*Soon after, for a few days, Salou searched his orchards for a snake. Finally, Salou heard the sound of a viper.*

*"Come, come, fat viper," he said.*

*"You are fat. Be the viper that gives his soup, his fat for my fat belly."*

*But as soon as the viper stung him, he began to scream in pain.*

*"It hurts a lot."*

*His blood festered. Salou could not breathe. He fall, and death took him. The villagers carried his body to the village.*

*Moral of the story:*
*The greedy man digs his grave with his teeth.*

# The Crow and The Guinea Fowl

One morning, the lion called all the sauriens of the earth unexpectedly and challenged them.

"I give you one day", he said, "to compose a nightingale song. My daughter Nima is no longer a baby. she wants a husband. Whoever comes to compose this song will marry this girl."

While all the sauriens were trying their turn, the crow had isolated himself in his cage. He then tried to express himself. He tapped himself and called for help. That's how he got a light.

With a cotton cloth, the crow easily placed a small tie on his neck and went to the front.

The guinea fowl, who was back after five days of absence, entered the competition. She had gone to her father's funeral.

The crow, who wanted to win, told the guinea fowl a few lies.

"I'll give you one day," he said, "to sing a buffalo song. The girl Nima is no longer a child, she wants a husband. Whoever comes to sing this song will marry the girl."

*The guinea fowl proceeded in the same way and did not reach his end. When it was the crow's turn, the crow got up, gently took the microphone, opened his mouth, and immediately sang the song. All the other sauriens were astonished. The happy him congratulated the winner. He kept his promise.*

*Since that day, the crow had a white neck.*

*"We can! We can!", shouted the guinea fowl while running after the crow.*

*This one flees. He opens his mouth, crying,*

*"Con! Con!" to make fun of the guinea fowl.*

# The Death of Bouki

*There was a time when the king of the jungle organized a giant battle. The winner had to kill his opponent and take him.*

*On the first day of the battle, Bouki's wife killed Gazelle and took her home.*

*The hare killed the partridge and took it home. Bouki's who was back after ten days of absence, went into a trance. She had gone to her father's funeral.*

*"Instead of bringing down a big game, this is what you bring us. Didn't you find the crocodile or the hippopotamus in the area?"*

*And the hyena, in turn, went away.*

*"Then I'm coming. I'll take a cart and come."*

*She arrived. From search to search, she met the crocodile. Unfortunately, the crocodile knocked her to the ground. Bouki was covered in dirt. When the crocodile was about to pounce on Bouki, she ran away at he speeds of her feet. What to do to bring her back? while she was walking quietly, she came across a young crocodile crying his eyes out.*

"Little croc..., What's wrong with you?"

"Me? I lost my mother, killed in a battle by a hyena."

"Really?"

"And if you doubt it, I can take you to see the corpse."

"Do it quickly, please," cried the hyena.

The young crocodile was very happy and took Bouki to his mother. Then, he presented him the corpse. Bouki's slowly approached the corpse.

"Wonderful!"

She immediately got on his back. There, she slowly stared at the young crocodile. As soon as she finished, mama croc... pounced on the hyena.

"I chose you."

The young crocodile helped his mother, and they killed Bouki.

# The Hare and The Child

*A long time ago, Leuk the Hare used to go to neighboring villages to nibble on the crops buried in the granaries.*

*As usual, the hare would go to an old man's yard and eat the bags of peanuts when he went to the field with his wife.*

*One day, having noticed the damage done to his granaries, the old man decided to leave his child at home and went to the field. The same day, Leuk the Hare came into the yard and greeted the child.*

*"Your father asked me to come and finish a bag of peanuts."*

*The child challenged the hare, who finally managed to convince him. In the evening, when the old man and his wife returned from the fields, they found that an attic had been visited. But the child informed his parents that after they left, an animal with floppy ears had come into the yard and stolen a bag of peanuts.*

*After the child's speech, the old man threatened him that next time he should do everything to stop the hare. The next morning, after leaving for the field, the hare returned, greeted the child, and wanted to eat another bag of peanuts.*

*Taking advantage of this opportunity, the child opened the attic, and when Leuk the Hare entered, he closed the door, waiting for his parents to come.*

*When his parents returned, they went to pick up the hare, and the old man tied him up and hung him on a shea tree branch to await his execution.*

*Taking advantage of the absence of his executioners, the hare who saw Bouki the hyena passing by called out to him and said,*

*"Friend Bouki, an old man gave me his daughter in marriage. and I refused his proposal for which I am attached to this branch."*

*Without much thought, Bouki laughed and asked to replace Hare as such an opportunity was rare in life. Bouki lowered the Hare and took his place, still hanging on the branch.*

*At this time of the execution, the old man and his child came out holding two clubs, a hot iron, and three knives each. From the top of the tree, Bouki was jumping up and down and impatiently waiting for his new wife.*

*When they arrived at the site, the old man noticed that their enemy had become large. Without delay, he raised the club and hit Bouki, who screamed with all his strength.*

*Returning to the charge, the boy burned Bouki's kidneys, who opened his mouth wide.*

*At the third time, the old man hit the rope, which broke, thus freeing Bouki, who fled with all his legs in the direction of the forest while uttering insults to Leuk the Hare and swore to settle his accounts with this little rascal.*

# The Man and The Woman

*A man had a wife. He said that the woman was worth a thousand barrels of gold. He talked about his wife to everyone. What people did was to admit what he said.*

*"As much as I love my wife. As much as she loves me. Is there that person across the earth who can turn away my wife's love?"*

*"I've never seen that. And i won't see that. Every day, she reassures me that if I die, she will follow. She only care about me, only to me alone."*

*"Can I believe in such love?"*

*The answer, I'm going to say no. The rest confirms the given position.*

*It was one day when the king learned that there was a man whose wife loved the latter as the mare loved her foal and was not ready to deny him milk, even if the sky fell on his head. The king looked around. He sent for the man. The man came. The king asked him this question.*

*"Man, What have you done to make your wife love you so much."*

*The man answered him,*

*"I have done nothing. It seems that it is the woman who loves me. I even told her my personal secret. She jealously guarded it. Ah, What a woman I had!"*

*The king looked heartily at the man.*

*"But you are not like the other man of my kingdom. For everyone, his wife is a bitch. How happy I am with you. You deserve a princess, but only if your wife agrees."*

*The man is forever satisfied. He went to see his wife, who stayed at home. The woman says nothing about this. She remained humble. The man goes to see the king.*

*"My king, my wife did not say a word. He who does not say a word, consents where is the princess?"*

*"There she is! Take her to your house."*

*The man arrived at the house accompanied by his princess and found his wife sitting.*

*"Here is your co-wife."*

*He pointed to the princess. The woman saw that her husband really took a wife. She jumped with surprise.*

*"It is because I protect your secret well that you do this to me."*

*She went inside and took the man's secret and threw it on the floor. The man turned into an animal and went into the bush.*

*That's how she lost her husband. So did the princess.*

# The Three Scholars

*Once upon a time, there were three scholars who had long been recognized for their knowledge. The knowledge of these men was immense. The people who lived in a large village liked to sit at their front door. They needed their advice before making a decision.*

*These scholars studied the lives of the villagers. They had saved the lives of many people. After a rather remarkable ascension, a king came to call them. He was the king of a kingdom: Tere.*

*The king took the three scientists to his home. They were well received.*

*That day they ate their meal with a good skewer of beef. The three scientists helped the king. They improved him with all their knowledge. The king was seduced the same day. He decided to reward them. For this, he called upon the three scholars.*

*"I give you the choice," he said to them. "of what you want."*

*"Go, my sons. You have more knowledge than a white man who comes from Europe."*

*He spoke to them as to comrades. Some time later, the three scholars began to talk. The first one settled down.*

*"You will give me, sire, a gourd filled with milk. I will drink. It is very good for the night."*

*"Let's give milk to this scientist," replied the king.*

*It was the second's turn.*

*"You will give me, Sire, a bottle filled with honey. I will drink. It is very good for the night."*

*"Let this scholar be given honey," replied the king.*

*Finally, the third scholar said,*

*"You will give me, sire a drapper girl, a rare beauty from the village. I will have a good time. It is very good for the night."*

*The king replied,*

*"Let them give this scholar a clean-cut girl, a rare beauty from the village."*

*That night, the king slept soundly. The next day, the king got up and wore his best boubou to visit the scholars. To his astonishment, he saw that the three scholars had not cut their target. The king called them.*

*"I see that not all the target are cut," said the king.*

*The first one to receive the gourd filled with milk came forward and said,*

*"Sire, you gave me a gourd filled with milk; This is why I did not drink the milk: this milk smells like a bitch."*

*The king asked that the milkman be taken away. The milkman was fetched and peacefully presented himself to the king.*

*"Where did you get the milk?," asked the king.*

*"The breeder gave it to me."*

*The king asked that the farmer be taken away. They went to get him, and he came to the king.*

*"Where did you get the milk?", the king asked.*

*"My sheep gave it to me. My dog raised it when she was motherless."*

*The king looked at the scientist. Now he understood everything.*

*It was the second scholar who was trying to speak too,*

*"Sire, you gave me a bottle full of honey. This why I did not drink it. This honey smells like death."*

*The king asked for the donor to be taken away, who peacefully presented himself to the king.*

*"Where did you get the honey?", asked the king.*

*"The beekeeper gave it to me."*

*The king asked that the beekeeper be taken away. The beekeeper was fetched and peacefully presented him self to the king.*

*"Where did you get the honey?", the king asked.*

*"The beehive gave it to me, the beehive of the baobab. There is a graveyard in the corner. That's all."*

*The king looked at the scholar. Now he understood everything.*

*It was the turn of the third scholar. He walked towards the king.*

*"Sire, you have given me a dashing girl, a rare beauty from the village. This is why I did not sleep with the girl; this girl is the result of a mixture of genders, said to be an illegitimate child."*

*The king asked asked that the parents be taken away, who peacefully presented them selves to the king.*

*"I would like to know where you found the girl?"*

*"It was my wife who gave her to me," replied the father.*

*"Don't argue," said the mother in a stern tone.*

*"This is not your daughter. I got the wrong pregnancy."*

*The king looked at the scholar. Now he understood everything.*

*The king had shaken his head. I still see.*

*"How learned and quick you are! I wish I could give my daughter in marriage to a great and gentle scholar. The choice is difficult. You have great talent as a scientist.*

*Of the three scholars, who should marry the princess?*

# The Two Hunters

*Two hunting brothers went out hunting.*

*They walked for a long time through the fields, searching the bushes and the caves, but found no wild animals. Tired of not being able to get away with it, the two hunters set out again for the village.*

*On the way, the older one saw a bush. Inside, what did he see? A big snake. He continued on his way.*

*The two hunters were already at the entrance to the village when the older one said to the younger one:*

*"I beg you to accept my apologies. I will return in a moment."*

*He then withdrew to the countryside, killed the snake, and took it away. As he walked towards the village, on the way, he heard a mysterious voice commanding him,*

*"I order you to let me go! Don't argue about it. It is the snake."*

*"I hear talking, but I don't know yet, said the hunter."*

*"How bad for you! You'll die for sure!"*

*Scared, the hunter got rid of his game and ran away. The younger hunter, who had retraced his steps and orchestrated this stratagem, took the snake away.*

# The Misadventures of
Bouki and The Dog

*In the past, the dog was a wild animal. How did he manage to return to the home of men? Read this story.*

*A long time ago, the animals of the bush led a disorderly life. To put an end to it, the lion gathered his bush brothers and asked them to build a school. This would allow their children to be better educated.*

*Upon hearing the news, all the animals agreed, and within a week, a large building was constructed. A contest was held.*

*Bouki and the dog became the two masters of this school. They took an oath before the lion. A week before the start of the school year, all the animals had already registered their children. At first, everything was going well.*

*At a certain point, Bouki and the dog started to eat the students. The hare soon sensed this. He asked all the parents to remove their children. The animals rejected the hare's proposal. The hare went to collect his children.*

*One day, around ten o'clock, all the parents were surprised not to see the children return.*

*Meanwhile, Bouki and the dog decided to sell all the children. Informed, the animals came to the school. Several children were not there. The dog, who had heard the people, took the key to the field.*

*He was chased but finally managed to return to the village of men. As for Bouki, she was horribly beaten. It is since this day that she has spine twisted.*

*Born in Burkina Faso, Younoussa SEGDA is a young Certified teacher who served in the school of Sangabouli in the basic education district of Bittou, Boulgou province in Burkina Faso. He holds a literary BACCALAUREATE A4 series. Passionate about storytelling and music, and a student of Modern Letters at the University of Ouagadougou, Younoussa SEGDA is now living in the United States where he is pursuing his studies.*